Tac's Turn

Tac's Turn

by Ruth Yaffe Radin

illustrations by Gail Owens

Troll Associates

For my aunt,
Anne E. Yaffe

A TROLL BOOK, published by Troll Associates,
Mahwah, NJ 07430

Published by arrangement with Macmillan Publishing Company, Inc.
For information address Macmillan Publishing Company, Inc.,
866 Third Avenue, New York, New York 10022.

First Troll Printing, 1988

Printed in the United States of America.

10 9 8 7 6 5 4 3 2 1

ISBN 0-8167-1319-7

Contents

1
Not Being Sure

TAC'S island seemed far away. We had already left Virginia, and the sign coming up said WILMINGTON—125 MILES. We'd be out of Maryland by then, heading north to Pennsylvania.

"Hey, Tac," I said, "if you don't want to stay a whole week, you don't have to."

"I know."

"We could call your mom and tell her you're going home sooner."

"I know."

"Steven," my mother said, "we want Tac to stay with us."

His real name was Thomas Andrew Carter, but he was called Tac for short. We had met just a week ago, at the beginning of our vacation on the island where Tac lived all year. We had been together every day since then, and I did want him to come home with me for a visit. At least I thought I did while we were still on the island. But now I wasn't sure. Maybe he wouldn't like it in Pennsylvania. It didn't have ocean or bay everywhere you looked. Besides, Tac didn't have sisters. That would be another thing for him to get used to. And the way he talked was different.

I looked out the car window. Everything was flat, sandy flat, with scrubby plants pushing up behind the gas stations. The vegetable stands on the sides of the road sold melons and corn, corn and tomatoes, potatoes and melons—the same things at each one, it seemed.

"We only grow tomatoes," I said, almost to myself. "There's not enough room for other things." Tac would probably laugh at how small our yard was.

"But we have enough for a salad every night," my mother added.

"Do I have to eat it?" Tac said.

"Don't you like salad?"

"Depends on what's in it."

"Sometimes there's spinach and anchovies," I said.

"Do you eat that stuff?"

"The spinach but not the anchovies. I told you I didn't like them." I remembered the little fish swimming in the pool left from the storm on the beach, and I figured that gulls appreciated anchovies more than I ever would.

Tac tipped his army hat to the back of his head. "I'm not eating anything I don't want to." He tapped my father on the shoulder. "Just give me the money my mom gave you to hold for me, and I'll buy my own food."

"Steven," my father said, "you're making Tac worry for no cause."

I slumped down, not looking at Tac. Just because we got along on the island didn't mean we would back home. Tac didn't even know what a real hill was. I was going to take him ice skating at the indoor rink, too. He'd probably hate it but I'd make him try. He'd made me use ugly fish heads for baiting crabs. We'd caught twelve of them. If I hadn't met Tac that first night on my bike, I would have used chicken necks and only caught a couple.

"You have malls?" Tac asked.

"Sure."

"With those moving stairs?"

"Escalators?"

"Yeh."

"Sure."

"I went on them."

"What's the big deal?"

"Steven," my mother said with annoyance, "did you see any escalators on the island?"

I didn't answer. He was from another kind of place.

"If I like escalators," Tac started, "I like escalators. If I want to go down the up one and up the down one, I will."

"They won't let you."

"If I want to ride them all day," Tac continued, "I will."

"Why don't you two eat something?" my father suggested.

Tac's mother had packed cheese, bananas, and cookies. Tac's hand and mine grabbed hold of the cookie bag at the same time. I let go. They were Oreos, and if my mother didn't look, we could open them up and eat the frosting first.

"You get two," Tac said, and then took three for himself before closing the bag.

"Hey!"

"Hey, what?"

"How come you got three?"

"I'm older than you."

"Not by much." We were both going into sixth.

Tac smiled as he reached for the bag and handed it to me. "I just wanted to see what you'd say."

"You aren't funny."

"Yes, I am."

"All right," my father said, "both of you be quiet."

"I'm sorry, sir," Tac said in his most polite Virginia talk.

"You said something," I whispered.

"Shhhh!" My mother turned around, mad. "We have four hours to go."

When we pulled into our driveway, the tires mashed the crab apples from our tree instead of crunching oyster shells the way they'd done on the island driveway. Our Cape Cod's crisscrossed windows looked extra small compared to the big, sliding glass doors of the island house we had rented. We had only been gone a week, Saturday to Saturday, but it seemed much longer.

I looked next door. David would be away camping until late Sunday night. He had told me that before we left for the island. I wondered what he'd think of Tac.

Tac and I were the first ones in. We dumped the stuff sacks and beach towels in front of the fireplace. "We're home," I yelled.

Debbie's room was empty, and I ran down the hall to Elena's. "Hey, anybody home?" Tac wasn't following me. "C'mon. She's just my sister." Tac didn't move.

Just then Elena came out wearing her Wendy's uniform, except for the hat. She threw her arms around me. "I missed you."

"Don't hug me," I whispered, and wiggled away. "How come you're wearing that now?"

"I have to go to work in ten minutes. Where's Tac? I want to meet him."

I looked in the living room and he

wasn't there. As we were about to go outside, my mother came in.

She kissed Elena. "Was everything okay?"

"Of course."

"Where's Debbie?"

"At Sarah's house."

"Where's Tac?" I interrupted.

"Outside helping Daddy."

"C'mon," I said to Elena.

When she said "Hi" to Tac, he turned redder than I ever saw him before, and he tilted his army hat down over his eyes. Just then, coming from a distance and getting louder, we heard a noise in the sky. We all looked up.

"Those are Canadian geese." Tac smiled. "Just like at home. Look at their necks sticking out and that one not following the others, doing what he wants to do."

Tac took off his hat and smoothed his sandy-colored hair. "Just like me." He grinned.

I wondered what kind of a week it would be.

2
Tac's Discovery

WAKING up the next day in my own room made coming home from vacation all right. The slanted ceiling near my bed, the shelves with my running trophies an arm's reach away, and the posters of rock groups taped on all four walls made this my place, not a room for a week.

Even though it was nine-thirty, Tac was still asleep on the mattress in the middle of the rug. I swung my feet slowly off the bed and started walking around him when he caught hold of one of my legs. I stumbled against the door with a bang.

"I thought you were asleep," I said.

"I was awake before you."

"How come you had your eyes closed?"

"I was dreaming."

"About what?"

"Nothing."

"You don't want to tell me?"

"No."

We were getting to know each other pretty well, but there were still secrets to keep. Maybe someday there wouldn't be.

Tac stood up in his underwear. "You sure have a lot of junk in here."

"It's not junk. It's stuff."

He picked up the fossil sitting on my desk and turned it over in his hand. "Look at all the shells in it. Where did you get it?"

"At a quarry my dad takes his classes to on field trips during the school year. In the rocks there are leftovers of sea animals."

"There's ocean there?"

"Millions of years ago."

Tac sat on my swivel chair and spun around. "Could we go there today?"

"I'll ask." I wasn't sure if my parents would want to take us so soon after coming home. "You have to drive about a half hour toward the mountains."

"That's not far."

"I guess not. We could climb a trail, too."

"Is it steep?"

"When you get to the top and look down, the farmhouses and barns look as small as Monopoly pieces."

There was a knock on the door. "Wait," I yelled.

Tac dove under the covers again. "It's okay," he called.

Debbie opened the door as far as it would go before hitting the mattress. "Are you two ready for breakfast?"

Tac poked his head out from under the sheet. "What is it?"

"Cereal, eggs, juice. I don't know. You have a choice. Anyway, I had to come up here to get you."

My mother said she didn't want to go anyplace today, but my father said he'd take us. It was just right out, not too hot. We packed peanut-butter-and-jelly and tuna sandwiches, hard-boiled eggs, cheese, granola bars, apples, cherries, and cartons of juice for the trail. We put canteens full of water in the car, too. Tac fit into Debbie's hiking shoes and didn't mind wearing them, because they were just like mine.

Nobody else was at the quarry, probably because not too many people knew about it, except for teachers like my father. Slanted banks and mounds of loose rock rose from where we parked. They weren't too high or scary to climb, and chunks of rock were easy enough to pick up.

We went over to a gentle slope. "You have to look really carefully," I said. "Some fossils are better than others."

Tac was picking up rocks and throwing them down. "Nothing yet. Are you sure this is the right place?"

"Sure I'm sure."

He went off to another mound, and a few minutes later he called to me. "Come here, quick. I found something." I made my way over to Tac, and he held out his hand. "What's this?"

"Wow! Where'd you get it?" I called to my father to come over.

"Right here where I'm standing."

"Maybe there's another piece of it." And I started picking around in the rocks.

"Another piece of what?"

My father took the rock from Tac. "It's a mold of a trilobite."

"It looks sort of like a bug," Tac said.

"It was an ancient animal whose shell had three parts. It shed it when it grew."

"Like crayfish and crabs," Tac said.

My father handed the fossil back to Tac. "You have a real prize, Tac. It's not easy to find trilobites."

By the time we left the quarry, we each had a lunch bag full of fossils. Tac lined his up on the back seat between us. "Look at all those little shells, just like home." Then he leaned forward and tapped my father on the shoulder. "Can we eat now? I'm hungry."

"Help yourself, but leave some food for the hike."

We'd each finished a sandwich before we had gone another mile on a road where the trees stood close, keeping the sun out. Not a house or cabin was in sight. When we came to the beginning of the trail, my father parked at a turnoff near a small sign that said TWO MILES TO THE LOOKOUT.

"That's no big hike," Tac said as he put on the backpack that held his camera and the rest of the food. My father and I carried the canteens.

"It'll take a while to walk with all the rocks on the trail," my father answered. "But if you want to go faster than me, don't go so far ahead that you can't turn around and see me."

"This is where I got lost when I was little." I had told Tac about it while we were on his island.

"When you took the wrong trail?"

"Yep. You have to follow the yellow marks on the trees." And I pointed to a splash of paint about as high up as a middle-sized man.

Tac started walking, looking distracted as he turned from side to side, getting off the trail and kicking up dead leaves and broken branches.

"What's the matter with you?"

"I need a walking stick." Tac bent down and picked up a branch. He broke off some side twigs and tested it, leaning on it as he took a few steps. "This is good."

Tac was ready to go exploring. On his island, I'd been the one who was seeing new things. Now it was his turn. My father had gone ahead and was up near a bend in the trail, waiting for us.

It was rocky, and off to the side the trees weren't able to stand close together because of some big bare boulders that jutted out of the ground. We stepped onto one of them, and Tac picked at its sparkling crystals. "This is quartz, just like in the sand."

I read the small sign next to the rock. "It says this rock is sandstone."

"I told you," Tac said. "It's just beach hardened up."

We began to hike again and easily passed my father, but even with all the starting and stopping, the three of us got to the peak at the same time.

It was like going outside, walking into the open after feeling the forest all the way up. We went as far out on the big boulders as it was safe to go, and Tac stood staring toward the horizon with his walking stick straight up next to him. He looked like a real explorer.

"This is a mountain."

We both looked down at the farms striped green and gold from corn and wheat. On his island, Tac hadn't been able

to imagine anything higher than a hill.
There, the hills were more like mounds
covered with scrubby grass or pine nee-
dles. We had only one week, but I was
going to show Tac my part of Pennsylvania just the way he'd shown me his
island.

Two birds circling overhead called to
us. Tac looked up at them. "What are
they?"

"Hawks, maybe."

"They sure are big and black." And
then, as if remembering something important, he stepped from boulder to boulder over to where he had put down the
backpack. "I've got to take your picture."

Tac had us stand, looking out over the
valley. Then he handed the camera to my
father. "Now take a picture of me." He
stood straight, tipped his army hat back
on his head and held his walking stick. "I
want everyone back home to know I
climbed a real mountain."

3
Wheel Dealing

DAVID came over in the morning and looked curiously at Tac. "Why are you wearing a hat in the house?"

Tac tipped it back on his head and smiled. "It's a secret."

I started to pull Tac out of the room. "C'mon, let's get our sneakers on. Go get your bike, David."

"Why didn't you just tell him your brother sent it from the army?"

"I don't know David."

"He's my best friend here. I told you."

"Big deal."

Tac was going to use Elena's ten-speed while I rode my five-speed bike. Elena's was a boy's bike, so Tac didn't mind. I couldn't wait to see how he handled Pennsylvania hills. We had done a lot of dirt bike riding on his island, but I hadn't seen

one hill there you couldn't look past, un-
less you counted the dunes near the
beach.

Tac looked at the gearshift.

"When you go up a hill," I said, "you
use low gears. When you go down a hill,
you shift to high. And only change gears
when you're pedaling."

"I don't need to change them at all."

"Yes, you do," David said. "How come
you never used gears before?"

"It's flat on the island," I said. "You
don't need gears there."

David made a wide circle in the street
in front of the driveway. "I'll meet you at
the foot of Moffit. That's a hill to try."

Tac was getting impatient, too. "I know
how to ride. You don't have to tell me all
this stuff." And he swung onto the bike,
letting it coast out of the driveway. "I'm
just going to the corner and coming back
up."

"Hey, wait. Have you ever used hand
brakes?"

Tac didn't hear me, and I yelled it again
as I got on my bike to catch up.

"What did you say?" He half turned around.

"Do you know about hand brakes?"

"Of course. You just squeeze them like this."

The bike skidded. "Watch out," I yelled as Tac's front wheel hit the curb. He toppled into the gutter, and the bike came down on top of him.

"Are you okay?"

"Just get this stupid thing off of me."

I picked up the bike. "You squeezed the brakes too hard."

"I wouldn't have done it if you weren't yelling like a maniac."

"If you had waited a minute more, I would have shown you how they work."

"You don't know it all."

"Neither do you." Then I saw the blood running down his right arm and leg. "Are you okay?"

"It's nothing." And he smeared the blood with his hand, trying to wipe it away as he started limping up the street.

"We'll come back for the bikes," I said. "Are you really okay?"

"I said I was."

"We don't have to ride bikes."

"Will you just shut up!"

David came around the corner just as we got to my house. "Will you get the bikes? Tac fell." And I followed Tac into the house.

It wasn't as bad as it looked. My mother made a big enough deal about the scrapes and insisted on painting Tac medicine orange, but he only really needed two Band-Aids. The bike was in worse shape. David couldn't even ride it up because the front rim was bent.

"Elena's going to kill me," I said to Tac.

"Maybe we can fix it before she knows it happened."

I rolled the bike forward till the rubber brake shoes jammed against the rim. "We'll have to take it to Dan's to have it realigned."

"What'll he do?"

"He'll take the tire off, pound out the dents, and adjust the spokes."

"I have my money. Your father gave me five of it today. How long will it take?"

"Maybe forty-five minutes for the work itself, once they get to it. But I've had to leave my wheels a couple of days when they're busy, and Elena will be home from work at two. That's four hours."

"So what are we waiting for? Maybe today he can do it fast."

I took the wheel off, and we walked through an alley to save time. Garages opened onto the alley, and back fences and hedges closed in backyards where gardens, doghouses, and a few full clotheslines were more important than patios.

"I wouldn't want anyone to see my underwear hanging in the backyard," Tac said. "Do any girls live around here?"

"Melissa and Amy live on the corner. We'll pass their backyard."

"Does it have a clothesline?"

I looked at Tac, and we laughed.

Dan's shop was in an old house. Bikes leaned against the railing of the porch, making it look as if a dozen kids lived there. Just inside, wheels and frames hung from hooks, and bikes took up all but a narrow strip of floor.

Dan was putting on some forks, and we waited. After he tightened a bolt, he looked up. "How're you doing, Steve?"

"I need a wheel realigned."

"It'll be a while."

"How long?"

"Pete's not here today, so I'm really backed up. You can pick it up tomorrow, late."

"That's no good," Tac interrupted. Dan looked annoyed.

"This is Tac. He's staying with me this week."

"I fell off the bike, and it's his sister's. We've got to fix it fast before she comes home from work."

Dan listened with a little smile on his face. I knew he was wondering where Tac came from.

"He's from Virginia," I explained.

Dan offered his hand to Tac. "Pleased to meet you, Tac." Then he turned to me. "There's one other way we could get this done, considering this is a special case. You know bikes, don't you, Steve?"

"Sure I do."

"I'll let you do it here. If you have trouble, just ask. It'll cost you two dollars to use the tools and for the advice. How's that?"

It couldn't have been better. By noon we were finished, and there was still plenty of time to put the wheel back on before Elena got home. Tac rolled the wheel ahead of him along Union Avenue. "Maybe she won't let me ride it again."

"It was an accident."

"You think I can't ride a ten-speed."

"No, I don't."

"If Elena doesn't let me use hers, will you let me use your bike?"

"Sure."

"And you're not afraid of me crashing it?"

"You'd better not!"

Tac grinned at me. Then he looked ahead and suddenly stopped. "Why didn't you tell me Burger King was on this street?" The sign stood high up, just past the trees on the next block.

"We missed it when we went through the alley."

Tac started pushing the wheel along faster, making it wobble as I kept up next to him. "Be careful with the wheel."

"Here, you push it." Tac reached into his sock and pulled out three dollars. "This should get us started." And we turned into the parking lot and headed for the door.

4
Getting There

ELENA didn't mind letting Tac use her bike again. He rode it that afternoon till he was good at using gears. The next day we rode to the pool. It was toward the center of town. Tac didn't have any trouble with the hills on the way, but the pool was crowded and not much fun. Also, the chlorine made his scratches hurt, so we decided to leave early.

"Let's ride along the alley," Tac said, crossing the street.

I followed him. We didn't have to go right home. At first the houses were close together on each side of us. Farther along, there was more room between them. Finally, there was open land to the left of the alley. People planted gardens there that they didn't want in their yards on the other side. Power lines stretched over the gardens, and I saw where they came from.

"I know where we are now," I said. "Up ahead, near the power substation, there's a path going down to the canal."

"Are there boats on it?"

"Just canoes. It's like a park. There's even a dirt track between the canal and the river that runs next to it on the other side."

"I wish I had my dirt bike here," Tac said.

"Me, too."

"Will you show me the track, anyway?"

"You can't tell my mother."

"Why not?"

"We have to cross about six train tracks to get there."

"Do the trains come by fast?"

"No way. It's more of a switching yard, but I'm still not supposed to go near it."

We chained our bikes to a tree and started down the path, winding our way through honeysuckle, wild rose, and blackberry bushes. Partway down the hill we came to the storage tanks.

"There's propane in them," I said. "It

goes in pipes from the tanks down to the tracks. The railroad workers fire the propane in the winter to melt the ice and keep the switches open."

"Do you come here in the winter?"

"We skate up from the center of town when the ice on the canal isn't covered with snow. It's too slippery to come down this hill."

"You said we'd go ice-skating when I was here."

"Maybe we can go to the rink tonight."

We came to a clearing, and Tac stopped to look at the train tracks at the bottom of the hill. "Look at those open boxcars. Did you ever go into one?"

"No, but I've looked inside them, and they were empty."

"Not even any bums living there?"

"I haven't seen any."

"Look at that old warehouse with all the broken windows."

The path was almost like a gully now where the rain had washed the dirt away. We held our hands out for balance and slid down the steep part till it started sloping gently again through the grasses and wildflowers. When we got to the gravel road that ran next to the train tracks, Tac turned onto it.

"Where are you going? We can cross the tracks now. There isn't a moving train in sight."

"I want to see the warehouse first."

"It's just an old, run-down building," I said, following him.

When we got there, we looked through the wide openings that used to have doors. Dirt had washed in from rain, and a bird was flying frantically around the gaping, deserted space, seeming to look for a way out. There were dark corners, but in the middle of the floor there was a shadow pattern made by the sun coming through windows that held different amounts of dirty glass.

"Okay, we saw it," I said. "Now let's go."

Just then we heard loud snoring.

"Over there," Tac whispered, pointing to a man sitting propped up against the wall to the right. "Look at the stuff around him."

"Rags and garbage."

The man stirred and we ran out.

"We'll see the dirt track another time," Tac said as we reached the path.

I looked back toward the warehouse. "Another time," I agreed. And we quickly made our way through the grasses till we were on the part of the path that was hidden in the bushes.

We rode home slowly.

"Do you think he lives there all the time?" Tac asked.

"It would be too cold in the winter. Maybe he goes to the Rescue Mission."

"We don't have one of them."

"I wish we hadn't seen him," I said.

"Me, too."

We rode the rest of the way without talking. Nothing had worked right this afternoon.

That night, Elena liked the idea of going skating, so she agreed to take us to the rink. It was open from eight to ten and it wouldn't be crowded because it was summer.

When we got there, Tac said, "If I don't like it, I'm not staying."

"You'll like it," I said, holding the door open.

We walked into the dark lobby. There were about a dozen lights on over the ice, and a girl, a little older than Tac and me, was figure skating by herself. She bent in half and stretched her leg out straight behind her so she looked like a T-square with arms.

We bought the tickets and found a pair of rental skates to fit Tac. "Lace them a little loose around the toes, then tight around the ankles, and a little looser at the top."

More people started coming in. At exactly eight, all the lights went on and the music started. Tac stood up on the rubber mat near the benches, wobbled a little, and sat down. "Okay. Now you have to tell me what to do."

"Stand up again and this time keep the blades side by side. You'll be able to do it." Elena was already on the ice.

Tac pulled his hat down and lunged forward, stopping just outside the four-foot boards that surrounded the ice. He blew winter clouds, making it seem colder than it really was. "You go skate. I want to watch."

I glided onto the ice, then pushed off, heading toward Elena who was at the far end of the rink. I looked back toward Tac when I got there. He had stepped onto the ice but was still holding onto the boards.

I skated back to him. "Take your hand off."

"I'll fall."

"I fall lots of times."

Tac moved his skates forward, inching his way along, still holding on. "Keep your skates pointing straight ahead."

"Get lost." Tac turned toward me and fell. "See what you made me do?"

Just then, Elena skated up, tried a T-stop, and fell, too. Tac was still sitting on the ice. "Turn onto your hands and knees and then get up," she said. I decided to skate away.

I bent my front knee so that I could press down and away with my back leg. I did it again to work up speed. I raced around the rink, passing Tac twice. Elena

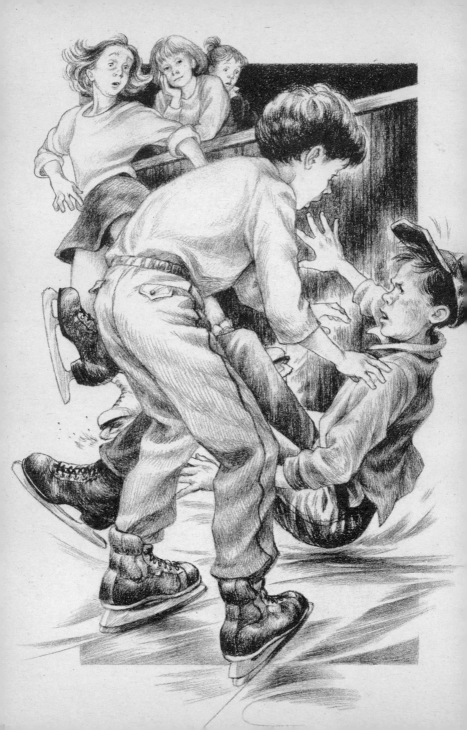

was still with him and he wasn't holding on. I kept going, weaving back and forth between the slower skaters. On my third turn around, I slowed when I passed Tac.

"Hey, wait for me," he called, pushing and gliding away from the boards, working with stubbornness to keep his skates going where he wanted them to go. "I can do it. See, I can do it."

"Do you want to go around the rink?"

"That's a long way."

Elena came up next to him. "I'll hold your hand."

Tac turned red and pulled his hat down over his face to hide it. "I can do it by myself." And he pushed off, skating unsteadily ahead of us. The day was going to end just fine.

5
Night Mystery

IT was hot in the morning, a real steamy July day. We had breakfast at the picnic table and let our bare feet brush the grass. It was pretty long. I'd have to cut it today with our old hand mower.

"Do you get paid?" Tac asked.

"It's sort of part of my allowance."

"I'll help."

"You have to really push." Tac had a riding mower at home.

We took turns, each doing two rows up and two rows back. David was out cutting his lawn, too. I thought about how hot it would be in my room later on. Maybe we could all sleep out in the tent tonight.

David liked the idea. "We could play soccer."

Tac gave him a funny look. "At night?"

"Mrs. Williams keeps a spotlight on for a while so robbers won't come."

"We have a policeman on my island," Tac said. "Tom's father."

"Just one?" David asked.

"Maybe there's more to steal on the mainland."

The three of us went swimming in the afternoon. Tac's scratches didn't bother him, and even though it was crowded at the pool, we had a good time.

After dinner, Tac and I put up the tent, facing it toward the woodpile. It wasn't exactly wilderness, with houses all around, but it was a good enough excuse to use flashlights and stay up late. In a little while, David came over with his Walkman.

When it should have been dark, the yard was half-lit from Mrs. Williams's spotlight, so we kicked the soccer ball around a little while. When she turned the light off, we had a snack and went inside the tent.

"I get the middle," Tac said. "Everywhere else I bump my head.'' He was much taller than David and I were.

We spread out the pads and put the open sleeping bags on top of them. I unzipped a side window and flopped down under it.

''I'll tell you a story,'' Tac said, ''about pirates.''

The walls of the tent flapped and billowed like sails on a boat, as if to set the mood.

''A long time ago,'' Tac started, ''a pirate called Blackbeard . . . .''

''Wait a minute,'' David interrupted, ''wasn't it Bluebeard?''

''No,'' Tac said, ''that was someone else. Anyway, a long time ago, when there were way more coon and deer and fox than people on my island, Blackbeard, a mean critter with a black beard . . . .''

''That's obvious.''

Tac glared at me. ''Be quiet.''

''Blackbeard sailed up and down the coast robbing and killing and being mean and no-good. The winds would blow and the water would shift and any bark or brig that got hung up on a shoal was like a trapped animal waiting to be killed."

"Bark?" David asked.

"A sailing ship with a lot of masts."

"What's a mast?"

"Just listen."

"But what's a mast?"

Tac looked at me. "Your friend is dumb."

"Just tell him. You had to tell me last week, too."

"A mast is the pole that comes up from the keel that you rig the sails to. Now let me finish."

"Wait," I said. "What's a keel?"

"It doesn't matter."

"Then what's a shoal?"

"A sandbar."

"Anyway, Blackbeard stole up from Carolina with the current and there was a schooner carrying gold and silver and molasses trapped on a shoal, just waiting for him."

"Molasses?"

"It was there," Tac shouted at me.

"Hurry up, Tac," David said. "They're

having a giveaway on EZ93 at ten-thirty, and I want to listen."

I turned onto my stomach. "I know what happened."

"No, you don't."

Just then a flashlight shone in. It was my father. "Is everything all right?"

"I'm trying to tell a story."

I sat up. "Blackbeard is going to rob the ship and hide the silver and gold on Tac's island. Then he's going to eat the molasses and get all sticky. Is that what you were going to say?"

"Never mind."

"Don't stay up too late, boys. We'll leave the back door open."

David tuned in EZ93.

"You made me come here," Tac said to me.

"You wanted to."

"You don't know the whole story."

"About Blackbeard?"

"He had fourteen wives, and one of them was on my island."

"What was her name?"

"Be quiet," David said. "I want to listen. They're giving away a case of Coke to the first caller who can tell who led the National League in RBI's in 1984. I bet it was Schmidt."

David was partly right. Mike Schmidt and Gary Carter each got 106. Two callers said Schmidt. Then another one named both and got the Coke.

We fell asleep on top of the bags, just far enough apart so as not to bump into each other. Later, when I felt a hand shaking my shoulder, I knew it wasn't an accident.

"Wake up," David said. "Tac isn't here."

"He probably went to the bathroom." And I rolled farther away from David.

"No, he didn't. I already checked."

I pressed the light button on my watch. It was 12:26. I sat up and rubbed my eyes, trying to wake up. "How long has he been gone?"

"I don't know. I just woke up. Where do you think he is?"

I put my sneakers on and tucked the laces in. "We've got to find him."

Out in front, a few houses had upstairs lights on. The chestnut tree on the corner, with the street light shining near it, didn't look any different at twelve-thirty than it did at ten.

"Maybe we should tell your parents," David said.

"Don't be stupid."

"We wouldn't let him tell the story. I was more interested in the giveaway."

I sat down on the front stoop, and David sat next to me. "We have to figure out where he'd go at this hour."

"He'll get lost."

"I don't think so. I think he knew where he was going." Just then it came to me, and I jumped up. "C'mon. Tac went to Burger King."

"How do you know?"

"Every time we go anywhere, Tac wants to eat."

"Is it open?"

"I don't know."

The streets were spooky. The cars were either resting quietly next to the curbs or tucked in garages nestled against the sleeping houses. The shopping center was all lit up for nobody, and the white parking lines on the blacktop looked like open-sided ladders lying down for the night. We walked across them, picking the shortest way to Union Avenue. Burger King was lit up but mostly empty.

"There he is," I said, pointing to the front corner table. Tac had his back to us, but he was easy to recognize with his army hat on. "Let's go in."

"Wait. What are we going to say?"

"I don't know."

We pushed the door open and walked over to Tac's table. He looked up with his mouth full of a Whopper.

"Why are you here now?" I asked.

"Why do you care?"

"I'm sorry I kept interrupting your story," David said.

"Me, too."

"So what? I don't want to be up here, anyway."

"You want to go home?" I felt a sinking feeling inside.

Tac looked at me. "You don't know anything."

"What do you mean?"

"You talk funny. You don't know about boats. So what if you have mountains? I don't care. I'm taking the bus home tomorrow."

Tac got up with his empty cup and Whopper box and tossed them into the garbage. Without turning around, he went out, walking in giant steps to stay in front of us. David and I caught up.

"I don't want to talk to you two."

"I want you to stay," I said, really meaning it.

"Why?"

"Don't be so stubborn."

"We're sorry if we made you mad," David said.

Tac looked hard at me, then at David. "I'll give you one more chance."

We walked up the street without saying anything more until I saw my parents standing on the front lawn in their bathrobes. "Oh, no. Look."

"Let me do the talking," Tac said.

My mother rushed up to us as we got closer to the house. "Where were you?"

"You see, ma'am," Tac started, sound-

ing very polite, "I just wanted to go for a walk, and Steve and David didn't want me to be alone."

My mother didn't yell. Neither did my father. As we walked toward the house, my mother put her arm around Tac's shoulders. "You're not used to being away. I should have realized that. I'll tell you what. Tomorrow you'll call home and talk to your parents."

Tac pulled away from her, already thinking about what he would say. "I've got to tell them about the fossils and climbing the mountain and . . . ." Interrupting himself, he turned to my father. "Could we go to Philadelphia tomorrow, sir? You said we could go one day this week."

My father smiled. "Let's get through tonight first. Are you boys still going to sleep out?"

"Of course," Tac said, sounding like his old self.

When we finally got inside the tent, I said to Tac, "I can't figure out why we didn't get yelled at."

" 'Cause I said ma'am and sir. That's polite talk. You have to know how to talk to parents when you've been bad."

"Yes, sir," I said, and we went to sleep for the rest of the night.

6
City Mountain

TAC talked to his mom and dad first thing in the morning, and he didn't say anything about wanting to go home sooner than Saturday. We were going to Philadelphia today, after all, but first I had to practice the trumpet and take down the tent after the dew dried from it. By nine-thirty we were ready to go.

We drove up Prospect Hill, where the buildings looked almost as if they had to hold on tightly to the land to keep from falling down into the valley.

Tac looked out the window. "How do you ride a bike up here?"

"I don't."

"Don't you go to these stores?"

"No. Why should I?"

"Haven't you been in all the stores around here?"

"There are too many."

"But you know all their names?"

"No."

Tac settled back in his seat. "I've been in every store on my island, and I can ride my bike anywhere I want."

But there was just so far you could ride on Tac's island before coming to water, I thought. Here, there was always one more street. Maybe we'd try some new ones before he had to go home.

We went down the turnpike and got to the Philadelphia Zoo by eleven. Tac and I bought hot dogs and soft pretzels from a street vendor while my parents paid for admission.

"Your dad let me have ten dollars of my money before we left your house."

"To buy souvenirs?"

"That's what I told him I wanted it for. The real reason is to buy something for your parents because I'm staying with you."

"You don't have to do that."

"I know, but my parents reminded me this morning, and I'd better or they'll really be upset. That's one of the reasons they gave me so much money."

"What are you going to buy?"

"I don't know, but it's got to be a surprise."

"How are you going to hide it?"

"I'll just call it a souvenir and not show them till we get home."

Inside the gates, we were on our own. We went into the big cats' house and walked slowly by the cages.

"I wouldn't like to be in there," Tac said, "all cooped up. Look at that cheetah pacing back and forth."

"There's a little door at the back of the cage," I said, "so it can go outside."

"Not to be free, though."

"If it were free in its own kind of place, we'd have to go to Africa to see it."

We walked around outside, looking at the elephants, monkeys, and giraffes. Tac liked the birds best. They were everywhere. Peacocks dragged their tails behind them or spread them out in brilliant fans. Bright pink flamingos balanced on their spindly legs.

"What's over there?" Tac asked, seeing a crowd of people.

"The polar bears."

We walked on the path around hunks of man-made rock to where we could see through a window wall of a big tank of water. Just as we got there, a bear dove in, all white except for his black eyes, nose, lips, and paw pads.

"He's doing the dog paddle," Tac said. "Look at his feet. They're almost like flippers."

The polar bear turned and dove, then, moving his front legs around and around, came to the surface for air.

"It must feel good to be in there," I said. "It's getting hot." I looked at my watch. It was 12:40. There was just enough time to get some food and meet my parents at one near the entrance.

After we left the zoo, we headed downtown in the car, past the art museum with a million steps, and Logan Circle with all the fountains and flowers. Tac kept looking out the window.

"What do people do in those tall buildings?"

"Work."

"Doing what?"

"I don't know. Maybe there are banks in them. Are there?" I asked my dad.

He said yes. "And in a skyscraper there can be a lot of small businesses renting out groups of rooms or maybe a floor or two."

"I wouldn't like to stay in one of them all day," Tac said to me.

"You don't like to stay in any building all day. Anyway, you could leave for lunch."

Tac kept looking up. "What's it like to be on a top floor?"

"I don't know. I've never been up to the top of a skyscraper, either."

My father looked at my mother. "Maybe we could go up in an elevator and see. There are some office buildings near the Liberty Bell."

My mother wasn't sure. "We can't just walk into any building and take an elevator without asking if there's some sort of observation deck at the top."

"I've never been in an elevator," Tac said. "There's not even one at the mall on the mainland."

We found a parking space and walked to Market Street, where we stopped for a light.

"That's the U.S. Court Building," my father said, pointing across the street at a glass, steel, and red brick skyscraper. "We could try there."

Tac aimed his camera toward the top of the building. "I have to take a picture of this."

The glass of the lower floors acted like mirrors, and we watched ourselves walk onto the front plaza. Inside, the lobby was big and busy. Someone was being interviewed, and the newspeople and photographers were pushing in close. We watched.

"They're not going to let him get away," I said.

"If he wanted to," Tac said, "he could, just by moving back and then running up those stairs."

My father turned to my mother. "This isn't going to be as easy as I thought. The elevators are beyond those guards and metal detectors."

"Hey, look here," Tac said, and he started reading a sign aloud:

"No person entering or while on property shall carry or possess firearms, or other dangerous or deadly weapons. . . .

Did everyone leave the guns in the car?" he joked.

My mother turned red. "Don't say things like that, Tac."

"Let's just see if we can take an elevator up," my father said. We walked over to a guard near the metal detectors. "Is there an observation deck on this building that's open to the public?"

The guard smiled. "There are windows looking west when you get off the elevator. From the twenty-second floor, there's a nice view of the city. This is a public building, being a courthouse, but because of security, you'll have to get permission from the U.S. Marshal's office to go up. Just take the escalator to the second floor and turn left."

Tac was spinning his army hat on his

finger. I could tell he was thinking what I was. Why did grown-ups have to make a big deal about everything? We had to walk through a metal detector, and the change in my father's pocket made it buzz. Tac had to leave his camera with the guard.

In the Marshal's office, the secretary heard our story and made a call. In a few minutes, a Mr. Richards, the Superintendent of Court Security, appeared, looking very official with his walkie-talkie.

"We can't allow you to go up unescorted, but I'll be glad to accompany you," he said, when my father explained what we wanted to do.

We walked down the second-floor hall with Mr. Richards and stepped inside an elevator. "What are those dots next to the numbers?" Tac asked as we went up.

"Touch them," Mr. Richards said. "They're Braille symbols, so blind people can be sure they're pressing the right button."

On the twenty-second floor, the doors opened and we ran to the windows. The traffic on the street looked tiny, and we could see cars parked on the roofs of some of the buildings.

"Everything's stacked up in a big city," Tac said.

"What's that blue circle on top of that building?" I asked.

"A heliport," Mr. Richards answered. "There's a helicopter shuttle to and from the airport."

That sounded like fun to me. "You don't get stuck in traffic jams when you go that way."

"What's PSFS?" Tac asked, reading the letters on top of a skyscraper.

"A bank," my father said.

"And right here is a city mountain," Tac said, "and we didn't even have to hike to the top."

We all laughed, and Tac said, "Now I want to pick up my camera, see that Liberty Bell with the big crack in it, and buy some souvenirs. Right, Steve?"

"Right."

We all got back on the elevator, and Tac pushed the button, of course.

7
Rides

TAC bought my parents a souvenir Liberty Bell, which he gave to them that night. He also bought one for his parents.

It was the last full day before Tac would go home. We got on our bikes and left the neighborhood, crossing Eighth Avenue and heading down toward the racketball club. I was more used to this road by car than by bike, but with Tac visiting, we usually would keep riding without asking permission.

We stopped about twenty feet before a railroad crossing. "Where does that dirt road go?" Tac asked, pointing to the right.

"I never noticed it before." It curved around the edge of the grounds where a big office building stood.

"Let's find out."

We turned onto the road, walking our bikes. Red berries bobbed on the bushes, and butterflies chased one another in and out of hiding places. We kept going till we saw a NO TRESPASSING sign nailed to a big oak tree.

"Nothing's going to happen," Tac said, seeing the look on my face.

"How do you know?"

"We'll only go a little farther. Anyway, you should find out what's here. It's right near your house."

Tac was right. But just ahead we saw a beat-up sign on another tree: BEWARE OF DOG. We looked at each other.

Tac said, "Do you hear any dog?"

"No, but if we see a dog or people walking around, we're going to leave fast. Do you hear?"

"I hear you."

By now we each knew how much we could expect the other one to do.

We hadn't gone more than the distance of a home-run ball before the road ended at the beginning of an old homestead, all overgrown and deserted. There were three doghouses but no dogs. There was a shed with siding boards missing and a house that was stone, partly covered with stucco. A stone foundation with a few door frames still standing looked like the bottom of a barn.

We leaned our bikes against the shed. Inside its half-open door, we saw old clothes piled on old furniture, looking as if they had given up waiting for someone to come back for them. A bee flew out of the musty-smelling shadows, and we backed off.

"Do you think they grew something here?" Tac asked, looking around at the fields that were full of wildflowers and grasses.

"Probably corn. See those stray plants over there?"

We looked through the windows of the empty house at the fireplaces with doors and the kitchen sink with a water pump instead of a faucet. On the crest of the hill, away from the house, the office building stood watch in the present while we walked around the past. We could fix up the old homestead in our own minds, imagining what it had been like to live here.

Finally, we sat down on the front stoop

where kids had probably played a long time ago.

"Are you glad you came home with me?" I asked Tac.

"That's a stupid question."

"Why?"

"Because if I didn't like it here, I would have left."

I thought about Tac going to Burger King the night we slept out. "You're right. Will you come again?"

"You've got to come to the island first. That's the way it works."

"It won't be until next summer."

"That's a long time away."

"Come on," I said. "Let's go."

That night my parents took us to the bike races at the open air velodrome. Neither one of us was excited about it because it was the last thing we'd be doing together. But when we got there, an eighteen-speed, fourteen hundred dollar touring bike was on display next to the ticket window, ready to distract us. A sign said there would be a drawing for it. Tac and I looked at the bike, both wanting it.

"Save your ticket stubs," my father said, handing them to us.

We put them in our socks and ran up the steps to the walkway that circled the velodrome. A breeze blew the flags on the poles around the rim and brushed against us, too. We leaned on a low wooden barrier and looked down at the oval track. It was banked so it looked a little wobbly in shape even though it was made of cement.

"It's like a teacup that couldn't figure out what kinds of sides it wanted," Tac said.

Some racers were riding slowly around side by side on the tilted surface, talking to each other. More were in the center of the velodrome, where gently sloping macadam at the base of the track led to a grassy area and park benches.

My parents came up next to us, and my father handed us a program. "The first race is a sprint, one thousand meters."

When the gun went off, nobody pedaled in any hurry. That bothered Tac. "What kind of a race is this?"

My father explained. "They start off

slowly, almost getting in line. The leader pushes against the air and the ones behind don't have to work as hard. Now watch."

Just then, a rider in back went high up on the track, then dove down, picking up speed, and pulled ahead. Everyone else started going faster, too, trying to gain the advantage.

"They're going to crash into each other," Tac yelled above the cheering crowd.

It sure looked that way, but at the end of the race, everyone was still on a bike, going slower and slower till they all coasted down the banked track into the grassy center, like water going down a drain, only you could still see them.

We left my parents and watched some more races from different places on the walkway, but Tac didn't really like them.

"They dress funny," he said, looking at the racers, all wearing tight shorts that were shiny black and too long. "Those helmets look like the bottom half was sawed off. And it's boring going round and round a track. I'd rather ride on a road and then turn onto another road, not knowing where I'll end up."

"You know all the roads on your island."

"I don't know all the roads up here."

"Then you'll come back?"

"Of course I will."

"Maybe you'll win the touring bike, Tac."

Just then we heard the announcer say, "Tonight someone will win a fourteen hundred dollar touring bicycle donated by our good friends at the Champion Cycle Shop."

I reached into my sock and pulled out my stub—784.

Tac tried to get his, but it had slipped down to his foot. He pulled his sneaker off, then his sock, and shook out the ticket stub. It was 785.

"The number is . . . ." There was a pause. "The number is 427. Will the person with the winning number please come to the press box?"

Tac tossed his ticket aside. "I don't

care. You don't need speeds on my island, anyway." He stood there, not bothering to put his sock and sneaker back on.

"Now," the announcer continued, "check your ticket for an early morning ride tomorrow in the WLRV hot air balloon that has just landed in the soccer field to the west of the velodrome."

We looked toward the field and saw the balloon bobbing in place, pulling gently against the lines that held it down.

"Would you go up in that thing?" Tac asked.

"I won't win, anyway."

"Will the holder of ticket number 785 come to the press box? I repeat, 785."

I grabbed Tac's ticket from the walkway. "That's you!"

Tac took his ticket, not quite believing what he saw. "You have to go up with me, Steve." Then he started running with one foot still bare toward the press box.

I stood watching Tac for a second. Then I picked up his sock and sneaker. "Hey, wait for me," I shouted, and ran after him.

8
Tying Knots

WE checked with Tac's parents to make sure it was all right for him to go up in the balloon. He was allowed, and the ride was set for 8:00 A.M. That would leave plenty of time to get Tac to the bus station. He was taking a one-thirty bus home from State Road, Delaware.

"They'll let you go up, too," Tac said to me on the way over in the morning.

"I didn't win."

"If there's room, they'll let you. I'll tell them." Then he tapped my mother on the shoulder. "Could Steve go up, too, if they say he can?"

"Would you like to?"

"Sure."

The pilot introduced himself to my parents and told them that he was fully licensed and had been an instructor for nine years. Then he shook our hands.

"Just call me Bob," he said. "Are you boys ready?"

Tac grinned. "I've got my camera." Then he turned to me. "I didn't even have to ask if you could go."

My parents would follow the chase van that carried the crew. The van would try to stay close to the balloon, and we'd keep in touch with the crew by walkie-talkie.

Tac and I climbed into the basket with Bob. There was a tube going from one of the propane tanks in the basket to the burner above us. Bob fired it and a flame shot up about thirty feet into the balloon with a loud noise.

"What's that for?" I asked, backing up against the edge of the basket, which was just big enough for the three of us.

"Don't worry. It's supposed to do that. The flame heats the air inside the envelope, or what you call the balloon, and makes it light enough to carry us up." He fired the burner again, and the basket lifted from the ground. We started floating up. I held onto the suede leather wrapping on the edge of the basket and looked down.

Tac did, too. "Is it windy enough today?" he asked Bob.

"You don't want a lot of wind. It's just right now."

Bob fired the burner several times a minute, and we floated higher and higher. Houses kept getting smaller, and power lines looked like string. The golf course and Little League fields were big, bright patches of green. Swimming pools looked like bathtubs.

"I wonder what my island would look like from the air," Tac said, taking pictures in every direction. The rainbow-colored balloon that Bob called an envelope rippled gently, but the basket didn't even rock.

"We're going east now," Bob said.

"Look at those cows. We don't have any cows on my island, just horses and a few goats and chickens."

"And plenty of fish around it," I added.

"There's no ocean or bay as far as I can see," Tac said, looking around.

"There are rivers."

"They don't count."

"When you get home today, are you going to the beach?"

"Maybe."

"That's pretty soon."

We were quiet, not sharing our thoughts. The balloon floated low over some hills, and Tac stretched out his arm to pick a leaf off the top of a tall tree. Some people walking along a country road called to us, and we waved back. Tac took a picture of them.

After a while, Bob turned on the walkie-talkie and made contact with the chase van. "I'd like to come down in the field at the intersection of Mill Pond and Quarry roads."

We'll be there in five minutes," one of the chase crew answered. "We'll see if we can get permission from the owner for you to land."

Bob drifted toward the field. The chase van was in front of the farmhouse, at the edge of the field, and my parents' car was parked behind it. A voice on the walkie-talkie spoke to us. "You have permission."

Bob controlled the amount of heat in the balloon in order to let it come down. We descended slowly. Then we gently bounced and creaked to a stop on the stubble of the wheat field. The crew steadied the basket while Tac and I climbed out. Bob pulled a string that opened the top of the balloon to let air escape till the balloon fell on its side. Then we all squeezed the rest of the air out of it until the crew could fold it and pack it in a big canvas bag. The basket was lifted into the van, and the canvas bag went in, too. We thanked everyone and said good-bye.

Two hours later, we were on our way to the bus. Tac asked my mother if there was any string in the car.

She looked in the glove compartment and found some twine. "How's this?"

"It's okay. Now I need a scissors."

My father handed a fingernail clipper back to Tac. "Try this."

Tac clipped off a length of twine. "Now you watch," he said to me.

"What are you doing?"

"Next summer I'll be allowed to take a boat out into the bay. If you want to go with me, you have to learn your knots."

"Why?"

"For tying up a boat. And you have to listen to me when we're in the boat and not argue."

"I don't argue."

"Yes, you do."

"No, I don't."

"See?" Tac said. Then he tapped my mother on the shoulder. "Isn't that right? He can't argue when he's in the boat."

"Absolutely not."

It was easier not to say anything else.

We tied knots till we pulled up to the bus station. While my father parked, we went in with my mother to get the ticket.

The bus was due in ten minutes, and we waited for it outside. My mother gave Tac a bag full of food and more advice than I could imagine he'd need for the bus trip.

Tac gave her a big grin. "You're going to miss me."

My mother smiled. "We all will, Tac.

But you'll come visit us again, won't you?''

"Steve's got to come to the island first. That's what I told him."

The bus pulled in, and Tac was first in line. I stood next to him while he waited for the driver to take his ticket. "Will you write to me?" I asked.

"I don't like to write letters."

"But if I write to you, will you answer?"

"Maybe I'll call you up."

The driver took Tac's ticket, and he got on the bus. It was hard to see in through the dark windows, but I could tell from the army hat that Tac was sitting a couple of seats behind the driver. I waved, and he waved back.

After the bus left, we got into our car for the trip home. I reached for the twine that curled up on the backseat, and I started tying knots. Next summer, Tac was going to take me out in a boat, for sure.